Princess Peony

and other princess stories

Compiled by Tig Thomas

Miles
Kelly

First published in 2013 by Miles Kelly Publishing Ltd
Harding's Barn, Bardfield End Green, Thaxted, Essex, CM6 3PX, UK

2 4 6 8 10 9 7 5 3 1

Publishing Director Belinda Gallagher
Creative Director Jo Cowan
Editorial Director Rosie McGuire
Senior Editor Claire Philip
Senior Designer Joe Jones
Production Manager Elizabeth Collins
Reprographics Stephan Davis, Jennifer Hunt, Thom Allaway

ISBN 978-1-78209-215-5

Printed in China

British Library Cataloguing-in-Publication Data
A catalogue record for this book is available from the British Library

ACKNOWLEDGEMENTS
The publishers would like to thank the following artists who have contributed to this book:
Marcin Piwowarski, Jennie Poh, Kirsten Wilson, Mélanie Florian, Helen Rowe (cover)

All other artwork from the Miles Kelly Artwork Bank

The publishers would like to thank the following sources for the use of their photographs:
Cover frame: Karina Bakalyan/Shutterstock.com
Inside frame: asmjp/Shutterstock.com

Made with paper from a sustainable forest
www.mileskelly.net   info@mileskelly.net

Contents

Noel's Princess

An extract from
The Story of the Treasure Seekers
by E Nesbit

SHE HAPPENED QUITE ACCIDENTALLY. We were not looking for a princess at all just then, but Noel had said he was going to find a princess all by himself — and he really did.

Greenwich Park is a jolly good place to play in, especially the parts that aren't near Greenwich. I often wish the park was nearer our house, but I suppose a park is a difficult thing to move.

The day the princess happened was a fine hot day, last October, and we were quite tired with the walk up to the park. When we'd rested a little, Alice said, "I see the white witch bear among the trees! Let's track it and slay it in its lair."

"I am the bear," said Noel, so he crept away, and we followed him among the trees. Often the witch bear was out of sight, and you didn't know where it would jump out from. Sometimes it just followed.

We hunted the bear in and out of the trees, and then we lost him altogether. Suddenly we found the wall of the park. Noel wasn't anywhere about. There was a door in the wall and it was open, so we went through.

We went over the stones on tiptoes, and found another wall with another door on the other side. We went through that too, on tiptoes. It really was an exciting adventure.

There was Noel. He was standing looking at a little girl — and she was the funniest little girl you ever saw.

She was just like a doll, with a pale face, and long yellow hair done up in two pigtails. Her cheeks came high up, like little shelves under her eyes. Her eyes were small and blue and she had on a funny black frock. As we came up near to them we heard her say to Noel, "Who are you?"

"I'm Prince Camaralzaman."

The funny little girl looked pleased.

"I thought at first you were a common boy," she said. Then she saw the rest of us and said, "Why, are you princesses and princes too?"

Of course we each said, "Yes," and she said, "I am a princess also."

She said it very well too, exactly as if it were the truth. We were very glad, because it is so seldom you meet any children who can begin to play a game straight away without having everything explained to them first.

This little girl had a funny voice — she didn't talk at all like we do.

Then we asked her name, and she went on and on, I thought she would never stop. The first were Pauline, Alexandra, Alice, and Mary was one, and Victoria, for we all heard that, and it ended with Hildegarde Cunigonde something or other, princess of something else.

When she'd done, Horace Octavius said, "Well that's jolly good! Say it again!" and she did. We told her our names, but she thought they were far too short, so when it was Noel's turn he said that he was called Prince Noel Camaralzaman Ivan Constantine Charlemagne James John Edward Biggs Maximilian Bastable Prince of Lewisham, but when she asked him to say it again of course he could only get the first two names right, because he had made it up on the spot as he went along.

So the princess said, "Why, you are old enough to know your own name. You should learn it off by heart."

She was very grave and serious. Then the strange little girl asked us where our maids and governesses were and we told her we hadn't any.

"How nice! Did you come here alone?"

"Yes," said Dora, "we came from across the heath."

"You are very fortunate," said the little girl. "I should like to go on the heath. There are donkeys there. I should like to ride them but my governess will not permit it, so I cannot go."

"Never mind that," said Noel, "I've got a lot of money. Come, let's go have a ride right now."

But the little girl shook her head and said she was afraid it would not be correct to go against her governess's wishes.

So instead we showed her how to play

cross-touch, and puss in the corner, and tag. She began to laugh at last and looked less like a doll. She was running after Dicky when suddenly she stopped short and looked as if she was going to cry. And we looked too, and there were two prim ladies with

little mouths and tight hair. One of them said, "Pauline, who are these children?"

The little girl said we were princes and princesses — which was silly, to a grown-up.

The lady gave a horrid laugh, and said, "Princes, indeed! They're common children!"

The little girl cried out, "Oh, I am so glad! When I am grown-up I'll always play with common children."

And she ran at us, and began to kiss us one by one, when the horrid lady said, "Your Highness go indoors at once!"

The little girl answered, "I won't!"

Then the prim lady said, "Wilson, carry her Highness indoors."

The little girl was carried away screaming, and between her screams she shrieked, "Common children! I am glad!"

The nasty lady then remarked to us,

"Now go, or I shall send for the police!"

So we all came away very quickly, and when we got outside Dora said, "So she really was a princess."

"And I thought it was play. And it was real. I wish I'd known! I should have liked to ask her lots of things," said Alice. Horace Octavius said he would have liked to ask her whether she had a crown.

So we all went home across the heath, and made toast. When we were eating Noel sighed, "I wish I could give her some toast." We knew he was thinking of the princess. He says now that she was as beautiful as the day, but we remember her well, and she was nothing of the kind.

Princess Peony

By Richard Gordon Smith

Many years ago in Japan, Princess Aya was walking in her garden with her maids-of-honour, just before her wedding. She wandered down through her favourite bed of peony flowers to the pond where she loved to gaze at her reflection on the nights of the full moon.

When she was near the pond her foot slipped, and she would have fallen into the water had it not been that a young man appeared as if by magic and caught her. She

saw him briefly across the
water, then he disappeared.
The maids-of-honour had
seen her slip and a glimmer of
light but that was all.
But Princess Aya

had seen more. She had seen the most handsome young man she could imagine.

"Twenty-one years old," she said to her favourite maid, "he must have been a samurai of the highest order. His dress was covered with my favourite peonies. If only I could have seen him a minute longer, to thank him for saving me! Who can he be? And how could he have got into the palace gardens, through all the guards?"

After that evening Princess Aya fell sick. She could not eat or sleep, and turned pale. The wedding day came and went without the event — she was far too sick for that. As a last resource, her father sent for her favourite maid and demanded to know if she could give any reason for his daughter's mysterious sickness. Had she a secret love? Had she a dislike for her husband-to-be?

Her maid told him about the mysterious samurai. "Since that evening," she said, "our beloved Princess Aya has been sick, Sir. It is sickness of the heart. She is deeply in love with the young samurai she saw. There never was such a handsome man in the world before."

That evening the poor princess was more wearily unhappy than ever before. Thinking to enliven her a little, the maids sent for a celebrated musician.

The weather being hot, they were sitting on the balcony, and while the musician was playing, there appeared suddenly, from behind the peonies, the same handsome young samurai. He was visible to all this time —

even the peonies embroidered on his clothes could be seen.

"There he is! There he is!" cried the maids, at which he instantly disappeared again. The princess seemed more lively than she had been for days.

The next night, while two of the maids were playing music for their mistress, the figure of the young man appeared and disappeared once more. A thorough search was made in the immense peony flowerbeds with absolutely no result, not even the sign of a footprint.

A meeting was held, and it was decided by Princess Aya's father that a veteran officer of great strength and renown, Maki Hiogo, should try to capture the youth, should he appear again that evening. He arrived dressed in black to make him invisible in the dark night and hid himself among the peonies.

Music seemed to fascinate the young samurai. It was while music was being played that he had made his appearances. As the ladies played a piece called 'Sofuren', there, sure enough, arose the figure of a young samurai, dressed magnificently in clothes, which were covered with embroidered peonies.

Maki Hiogo stealthily approached the young man, and, seizing him around the waist, held him tight. But after a few seconds Maki Hiogo felt a kind of wet steam falling on his face. Still grasping the young samurai – for he had made up his mind that he would secure him – he fell to the ground.

As the guards rushed over to help, Maki

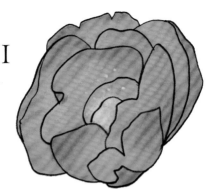

Hiogo shouted, "Come, gentlemen! I have caught him. Come and see!" But the man had disappeared, and Maki Hiogo only held a large peony in his arms!

By this time the king had arrived at the spot where Maki Hiogo lay, and so had Princess Aya and her maids-in-waiting.

All were astounded and mystified except the king himself, who said "Ah! It is as I thought. It is the spirit of the peony flower that took the form of a prince."

Turning to his daughter and her maids, he said, "You must take this as a great compliment, and pay respect to the peony. Show the one caught by Maki Hiogo kindness by taking care of it."

So Princess Aya carried the flower back to her room, where she put it in a vase of water and placed it near her pillow. She felt as if she had her sweetheart with her.

Day by day she got better. She tended the peony herself, and, strangely, the flower seemed to get stronger and stronger, instead of fading.

At last the princess recovered. She became radiantly beautiful once again, while the peony continued to remain in perfect bloom, showing no sign of dying.

As Princess Aya was now perfectly well again, her father could no longer put off the wedding. Some days later, the bridegroom and all his family arrived at the castle, and the next day he was married to Princess Aya in a great ceremony.

As soon as the wedding was over, the peony was found dead and withered still in its vase. After this, the villagers called Princess Aya 'Princess Peony' instead.

The Swan Children of Lir

By Thomas Higginson

This is a story from Irish
folklore. Erin is a name for Ireland.
The name Aodh is pronounced 'Eh'.

KING LIR OF ERIN HAD FOUR YOUNG children who were cared for by their stepmother, the new queen, but there came a time when she grew very jealous of the love their father had for them.

Sometimes there was murder in the stepmother's heart, but she could not bear the thought of that wickedness, so she chose another way to get rid of them.

One day she took the children for a drive in her chariot. There was Princess Finola, who was eight years old, and her three younger brothers — Aodh, Fiacre and little Conn, still a baby. They were beautiful children, with skin as white and soft as swans' feathers, and with large blue eyes and sweet voices.

Now, the wicked stepmother was of the magician's race, and she had magical powers. After they had journeyed for a short while they reached a large lake. The wicked stepmother told the four children that they could go and swim in the crystal clear water so they walked down to the lake and began swimming joyfully. Soon after, however, the queen took out her magic wand and cast a terrible spell.

One by one the children turned into four

beautiful, snow-white swans. The swans still had human voices, and so Finola said to the queen, "This wicked deed of yours will be punished one day. How long shall we be in the shape of swans?"

"For three hundred years on smooth Lake Darvra," said the queen, "then three hundred years on the Sea of Moyle, and then three hundred years at Inis Glora, in the Great Western Sea. Until St Patrick comes to Ireland, and you hear the bell, you shall not be freed. Neither your power nor mine can bring you back to human shape, but you shall keep your human reason and your speech, and you shall sing music so sweet that all who hear it shall listen."

She left them, and before long their father, King Lir, came to the shore and heard their singing. He asked how they came to have human voices.

"We are your four children, Father," said Finola, "changed into swans by our stepmother's jealousy."

"Then come and live with me," said her sorrowing father.

"We cannot leave the lake," she said, "or

live with our people anymore. But we are allowed to dwell together and to keep our reason and our speech, and to sing sweet music to you." So they sang to the king and his followers and lulled them to sleep.

When King Lir awoke he was determined to find his wife, the queen. He discovered she had returned to her father's palace and so the king journeyed there.

When he arrived, King Lir told the queen's father, King Bove, what the queen had done, and he was furious.

"This wicked deed," said King Bove, "shall punish the queen more than the innocent children, for their suffering shall end, but hers never shall."

King Bove asked the queen what bird, beast or devil she most hated, and she replied, "The demon of the air – the bat."

"So be it," said King Bove, who also had magical power. He struck the queen with his wand, and she became a bat. Legend says 'She is still a demon of the air and shall be until the end of time'.

After this, people used to come to the lake and listen to the swans. The happy were made happier and the sad forgot their sorrows. There was peace in all that region, while war filled other lands. Vast changes took place in three centuries but still the swan-children lived, until at the end of three hundred years they flew away to the stormy Sea of Moyle. From then on it was the law that no one should kill a swan in Erin.

Beside the Sea of Moyle they no longer

found the peaceful and
wooded shores they had
known, but rocky
coasts and wild water.
There came a great storm
one night, and the swans
knew that they could not
keep together. They resolved that if
separated they would meet at a rock called
Carricknarone. Finola arrived first, and took
her brothers under her wings. So passed their
lives until Finola sang one day, "The Second
Woe has passed — the second period of three
hundred years."

They flew out on the ocean, and went to
the island of Inis Glora. There they spent the

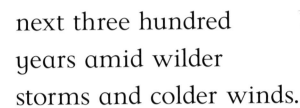

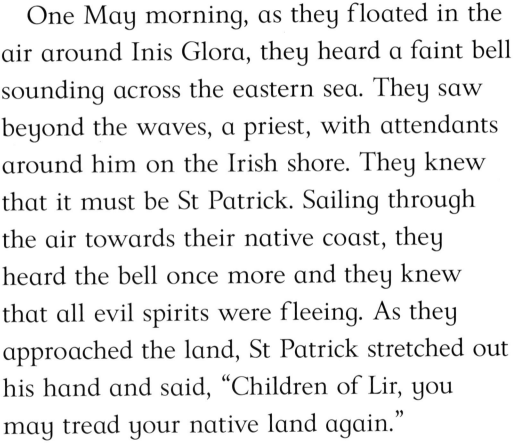

next three hundred
years amid wilder
storms and colder winds.

One May morning, as they floated in the
air around Inis Glora, they heard a faint bell
sounding across the eastern sea. They saw
beyond the waves, a priest, with attendants
around him on the Irish shore. They knew
that it must be St Patrick. Sailing through
the air towards their native coast, they
heard the bell once more and they knew
that all evil spirits were fleeing. As they
approached the land, St Patrick stretched out
his hand and said, "Children of Lir, you
may tread your native land again."

When they touched the shore, they
became human again, but they now
appeared old, pale and wrinkled.

And then they died, but, even as they did

so, a change swiftly came over them. They were children again, in their white night-clothes, as when their father King Lir, long centuries ago, had kissed them at evening. Their time of sorrow was over, but the cruel stepmother remains in her bat-like shape, and a single glance at her little face will lead us to doubt whether she has repented of her evil deed.

Ozma and the Little Wizard

By L Frank Baum

ONCE UPON A TIME there lived in the beautiful Emerald City, which lies in the centre of the fair Land of Oz, a lovely girl called Princess Ozma, who was ruler of that country. Among those who served her was a little, withered old man known as the Wizard of Oz.

This little wizard could do a good many things in magic, but he was a kind man, so, instead of fearing him because of his magic, everybody loved him.

Ozma decided one morning to make a journey to all parts of the country, so that she might discover if there was any wrong that ought to be righted. She asked the little wizard to accompany her on her trip, and he was glad to go.

So the two left the Emerald City and wandered over the country for many days. Stopping one morning at a cottage, built beside the rocky path which led into a pretty valley beyond, Ozma asked a man, "Are you happy? Have you any complaint to make of your lot?"

And the man replied, "We are happy except for three mischievous imps that often come here to annoy us. If strangers pass through the valley the imps jeer at them, make horrid faces and often throw stones at them for no good reason."

They told the good man that they would see what could be done to protect him from the imps and at once entered the valley.

Before long they came upon three caves, hollowed from the rocks, and in front of each cave squatted a strange little dwarf. They had big round ears, flat noses and wide grinning mouths, and dark hair that came to points on top of their heads, much resembling horns. One of them suddenly reached out a hand and caught the dress of the princess, jerking it so that she nearly fell down, and another imp

33

pushed the little wizard so hard that he bumped against Ozma and both unexpectedly sat down upon the ground.

At this the imps laughed boisterously and began running around in a circle, kicking dust upon the Royal Princess, who cried, "Wizard, do your duty!"

The wizard promptly obeyed. He opened his bag and muttered a spell.

Instantly the three Imps became three bushes — of a thorny stubby kind — with their roots in the ground.

"They can't help being good now, your Highness," said the wizard.

But something must have been wrong with the wizard's magic, or the creatures had magic of their own, for no sooner were the words spoken than the bushes began to move. Pretty soon they began to slide over the ground, their roots dragging through the earth. One pricked the wizard so sharply with its thorns that he cried out in pain.

Ozma sprang behind a tree and shouted, "Quick! Wizard, transform them into something else."

The wizard heard her, and grabbing from his bag the first magical tool he could find, he transformed the bushes into three pigs. That astonished the imps. In the shape of pigs — fat, roly-poly and cute — they scampered off a little distance and sat down to think about what to do next.

Ozma drew a long breath and coming from behind the tree she said, "That is much better, for pigs must be quite harmless."

But the imps were now angry and had no intention of behaving. As Ozma and the little wizard turned away from them, the

three pigs rushed forwards, dashed between their legs, and tripped them up, so that both lost their balance and toppled over.

As the wizard tried to get up he was tripped again and fell across the back of the third pig, which carried him on a run until it dumped the little man in the river. Ozma could not help laughing at his woeful appearance when he climbed out of the water and onto the riverbank.

The pigs tried to trip Princess Ozma, too, but she ran around a tree stump and managed to keep out of their way. So the wizard scrambled out of the water again and mumbled a magic mutter to dry his clothes, then he hurried off to help Ozma.

"This simply won't do," said the princess. "The pig imps would annoy travellers as much as the real imps. Please transform them into something else, Wiz."

So the wizard thought, then he changed the pigs into three blue doves.

"Doves," said he with a smile, "are the most harmless things in the world — the imps can't get up to mischief as birds."

But scarcely had he spoken when the doves flew at them and tried to peck out their eyes. When they shielded their eyes with their hands, two of the doves bit the wizard's fingers and another caught the pretty pink ear of the princess in its bill so that she cried out in pain.

"These birds are worse than pigs, Wizard," she called. "You must transform the imps into something that is not alive."

The wizard was pretty busy, just then, driving off the birds, but he managed to open his bag of magic and find a charm, which changed the doves into three buttons.

As they fell to the ground he picked them up and smiled. The wizard then placed the buttons in a little box, which he put in his jacket pocket to keep safe.

"Now," said he, "the imps cannot annoy travellers. We shall take them with us to the Emerald City."

"But we dare not use the buttons," said Ozma, smiling once more now that the danger was over.

"Why not?" asked the wizard. "I intend to sew them upon my coat and watch them carefully. The spirits of the imps are still in the buttons, and after a time they will be sorry for their naughtiness and may decide to be very good in the future. When they feel that way, I shall then restore them to their proper forms."

"Ah, that is magic well worthwhile," exclaimed Ozma, well pleased. "There is no doubt, my friend, but that you are a very clever wizard."